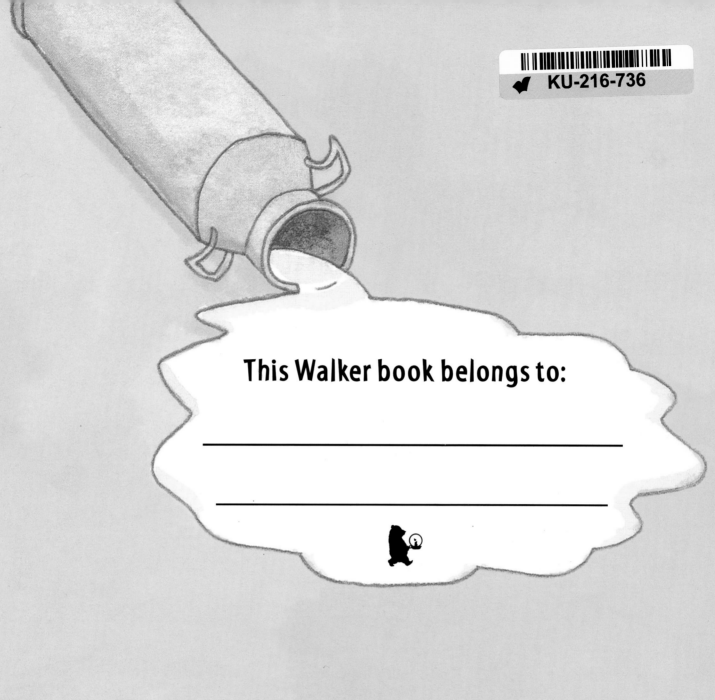

This Walker book belongs to:

_____

_____

For Andrew Nigel John — J.C.

For Ru — K.M^cE.

First published 1998 by Walker Books Ltd
87 Vauxhall Walk, London SE11 5HJ

This edition published 2010

10 9 8 7 6 5 4 3 2

Text © 1998 June Crebbin
Illustrations © 1998 Katharine McEwen

This book has been typeset in Myriad Tilt Bold

Printed in China

British Library Cataloguing in Publication Data:
a catalogue record for this book is available from the British Library

ISBN 978-1-4063-2632-1

www.walker.co.uk

Cows
in the
Kitchen

June Crebbin

illustrated by
Katharine McEwen

WALKER BOOKS
AND SUBSIDIARIES
LONDON · BOSTON · SYDNEY

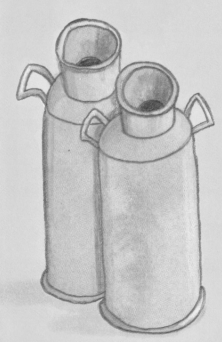

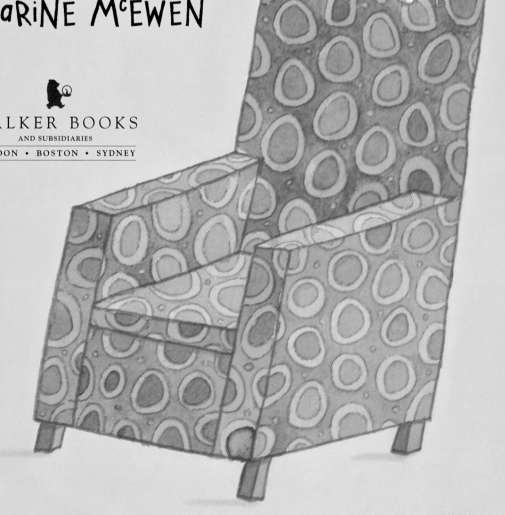

Cows in the kitchen, moo, moo, moo,
Cows in the kitchen, moo, moo, moo,

Cows in the kitchen, moo, moo, moo.
That's what we do, Tom Farmer!

Ducks on the dresser, quack, quack, quack,
Ducks on the dresser, quack, quack, quack

Ducks on the dresser, quack, quack, quack.
That's what we do, Tom Farmer!

Pigs in the pantry, oink, oink, oink,
Pigs in the pantry, oink, oink, oink,

Pigs in the pantry, oink, oink, oink.
That's what we do, Tom Farmer!

Hens on the hatstand, cluck, cluck, cluck,
Hens on the hatstand, cluck, cluck, cluck

Hens on the hatstand, cluck, cluck, cluck.
That's what we do, Tom Farmer!

Sheep on the sofa, baa, baa, baa,
Sheep on the sofa, baa, baa, baa,

Sheep on the sofa, baa, baa, baa.
That's what we do, Tom Farmer!

Farmer in the haystack, zzz, zzz, zzz,
Farmer in the haystack, zzz, zzz, zzz,

Farmer in the haystack,

zzz, zzz, zzz . . .

TIME TO WAKE UP,

TOM FARMER!

Out of the farmhouse, shoo, shoo, shoo,
Out of the farmhouse, shoo, shoo, shoo,

Out of the farmhouse, shoo, shoo, shoo,
Shoo, shoo, shoo, shoo, shoo!

Farmer in the armchair, shhh, shhh, shhh,
Farmer in the armchair, shhh, shhh, shhh,

Farmer in the armchair, shhh, shhh, shhh,
Shhh, shhh, shhh, shhh, shhh.

Lift the latch, shhh, shhh, shhh.

Push the door, shhh, shhh, shhh.

Creep down the hall,

Shhh, Shhh, Shhh ...

THAT'S WHAT WE DO,

TOM FARMER!

More books by June Crebbin:

978-0-7445-4701-6

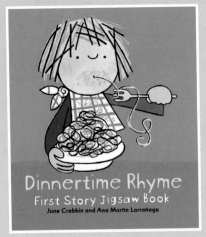

978-0-7445-7041-0

More books by Katharine McEwen:

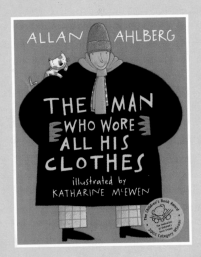

978-0-7445-8995-5

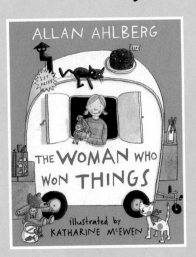

978-0-7445-9496-6

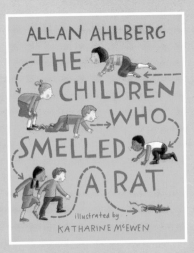

978-1-4063-0134-2

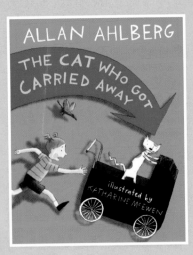

978-0-7445-9843-8

Available from all good bookstores

www.walker.co.uk